Witch, Witch
come to my party

By Arden Druce

Illustrated by Pat Ludlow

Published by Child's Play (International) Ltd

Swindon   Auburn ME   Sydney   St Catharines

© A. Druce 1991   ISBN 0-85953-781-1 (soft cover)   Printed in China
This impression 1998   ISBN 0-85953-780-3 (hard cover)
Library of Congress Number 91-29763
A catalogue reference for this book is available from the British Library

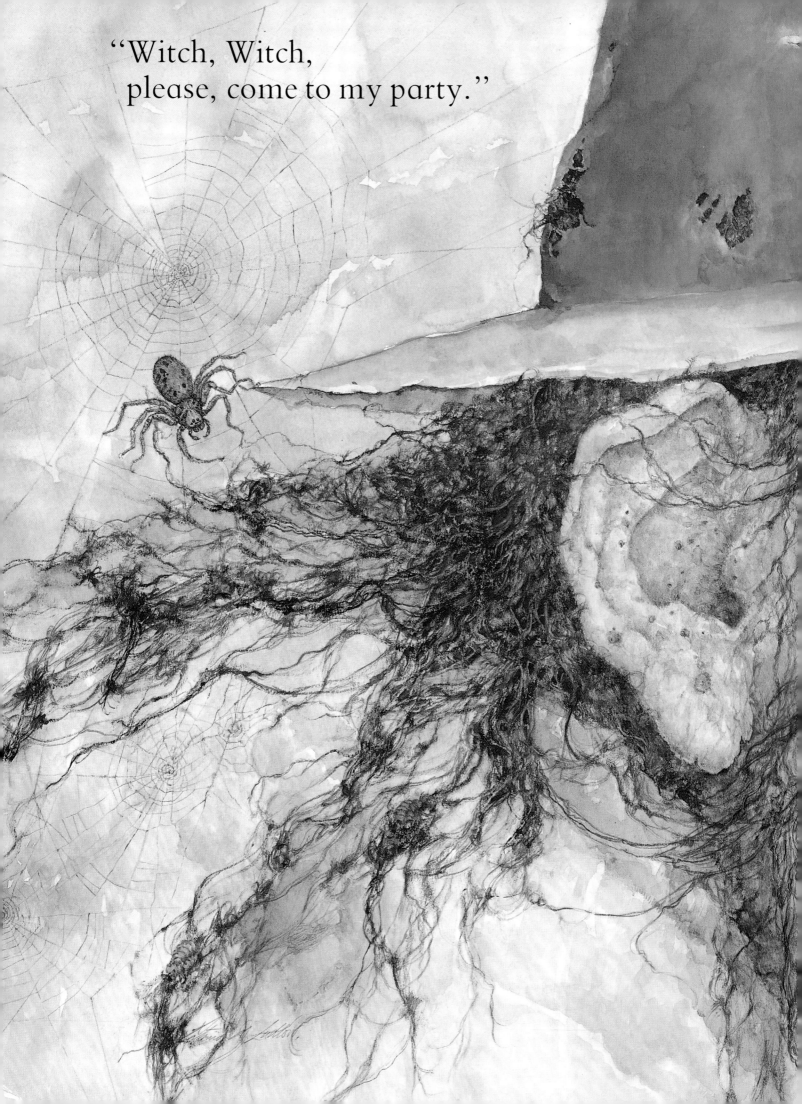

"Witch, Witch,
please, come to my party."

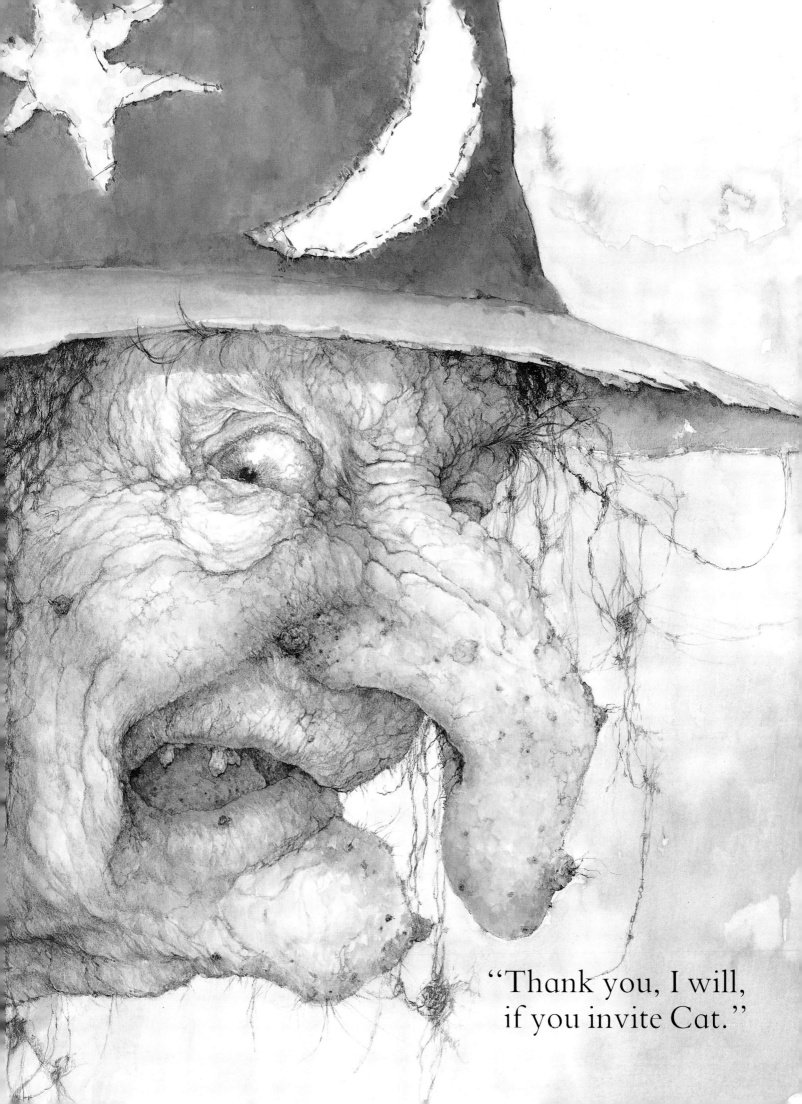

"Thank you, I will,
if you invite Cat."

"Cat, Cat, please, come to my party."

"Thank you, I will,
if you invite Scarecrow."

"Scarecrow, Scarecrow,
please, come to my party."

"Thank you, I will,
if you invite Owl."

"Owl, Owl, please, come to my party."

"Thank you, I will, if you invite Tree."

"Tree, Tree,
      please, come to my party."

"Thank you, I will, if you invite Goblin."

"Goblin, Goblin, please, come to my party."

"Thank you, I will, if you invite Dragon."

"Dragon, Dragon,
   please, come to my party."

"Thank you, I will, if you invite Pirate."

"Pirate, Pirate,
   please, come to my party."

"Thank you, I will,
if you invite Shark."

"Shark, Shark, please, come to my party."

"Thank you, I will, if you invite Snake."

"Snake, Snake, please, come to my party."

"Thank you, I will, if you invite Unicorn."

"Unicorn, Unicorn, please, come to my party."

"Thank you, I will,
if you invite
Ghost."

"Ghost, Ghost, please, come to my party."

"Thank you, I will, if you invite Baboon."

"Baboon, Baboon, please, come to my party."

"Thank you, I will, if you invite Wolf."

"Wolf, Wolf, please, come to my party."

"Thank you, I will, if you invite Red Riding-Hood."

"Red Riding-Hood, Red Riding-Hood, please, come to my party."

"Thank you, I will, if you invite Children."

"Children, Children,
   please, come to my party."

"Thank you, we will, if you invite Witch."